HOTEL TRANSYLVANIA

Welcome to DRAC'S CASTLE!

Adapted by Natalie Shaw

Simon Spotlight

New York London Toronto Sydney New Delhi

Sony Pictures
Animation

SIMON SPOTLIGHT

An imprint of Simon & Schuster Children's Publishing Division

1230 Avenue of the Americas, New York, New York 10020

This Simon Spotlight paperback edition June 2018

For information about special discounts for bulk purchases, please contact Simon & Schuster
Special Sales at 1-866-506-1949 or business@simonandschuster.com.

Manufactured in the United States of America 0618 LAK

10 9 8 7 6 5 4 3 2

ISBN 978-1-5344-1752-6

ISBN 978-1-5344-2561-3 [eBook]

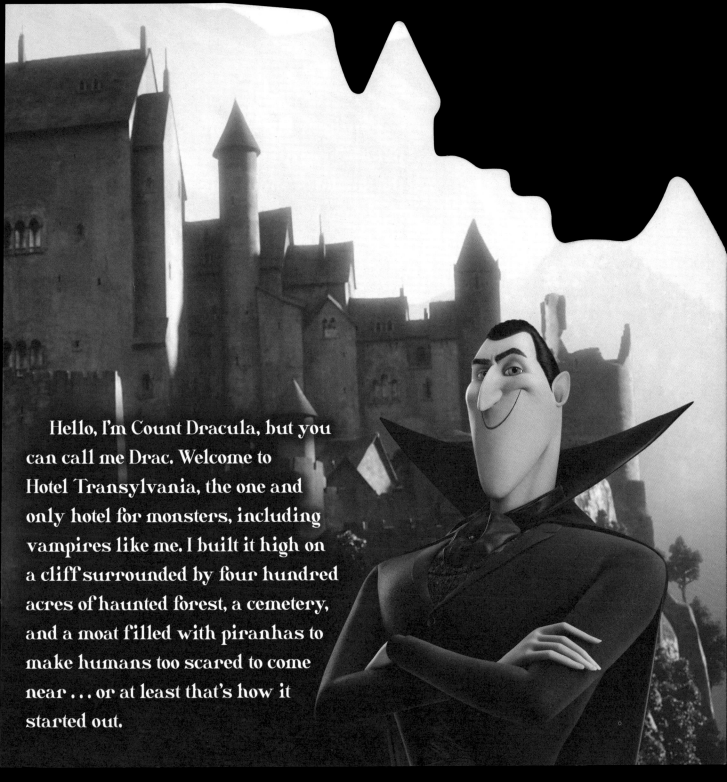

Hello, I'm Count Dracula, but you can call me Drac. Welcome to Hotel Transylvania, the one and only hotel for monsters, including vampires like me. I built it high on a cliff surrounded by four hundred acres of haunted forest, a cemetery, and a moat filled with piranhas to make humans too scared to come near ... or at least that's how it started out.

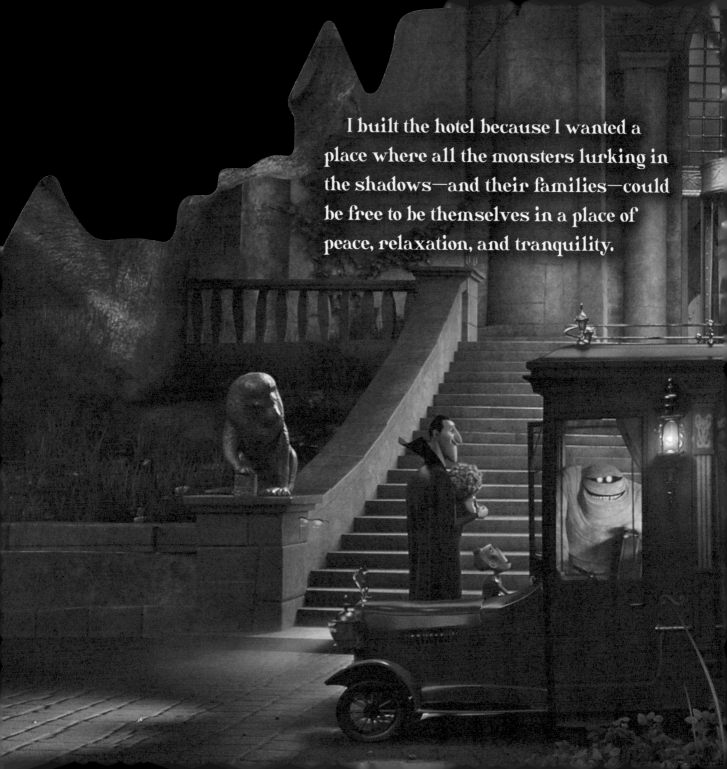

I built the hotel because I wanted a place where all the monsters lurking in the shadows—and their families—could be free to be themselves in a place of peace, relaxation, and tranquility.

From the moment we opened our doors, monsters came in droves in our zombie-driven cabs!

I was looking for peace and tranquility too—to keep me and my daughter, Mavis, safe from the outside world. Now we live at the hotel, and it has become a haven for monsters of all kinds...and hotel guests who are like family.

Are you ready to go inside? Follow me!

After you walk up the grand staircase and through the revolving doors, you'll arrive in the magnificent lobby. We spared no expense: That's why we have a top five-stake rating.

When you check in at the front desk, a zombie will give you your room key.

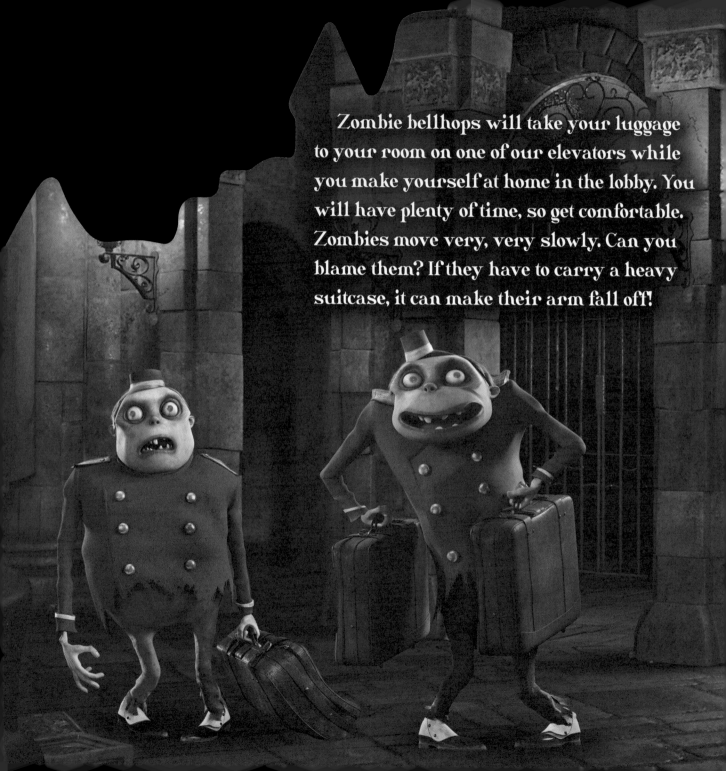

Zombie bellhops will take your luggage to your room on one of our elevators while you make yourself at home in the lobby. You will have plenty of time, so get comfortable. Zombies move very, very slowly. Can you blame them? If they have to carry a heavy suitcase, it can make their arm fall off!

While you wait, enjoy the entertainment from our mariachi band or try your hand at the pipe organ. It's spooktacular!

During your stay, you won't have to worry about a thing. If your wolf pup has an accident on the red carpet or chews through some furniture, a housekeeping witch will clean it up like magic.

If you feel a chill, you can warm your
bones by one of the magnificent fireplaces.
Just don't invite Frankenstein to join you—he
is terrified of fire!

Once you get settled in, you can even take a tennis lesson . . . but watch out for the coach. He tends to bury the tennis balls instead of hitting them. He can't help it: He's a werewolf. It's what they do.

Next you can take a dip in the moonlit pool! It's very refreshing, except when Murray the Mummy or Frankenstein does a belly flop.

If you get bored, you can find a book to read in our beautiful library or join in on one of our popular bingo nights there. It is so much fun!

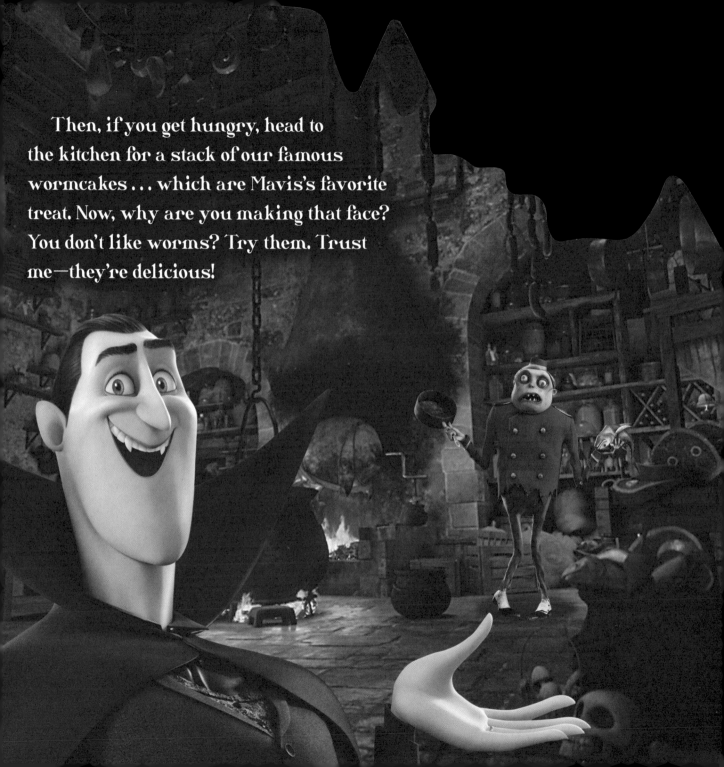

Then, if you get hungry, head to the kitchen for a stack of our famous wormcakes . . . which are Mavis's favorite treat. Now, why are you making that face? You don't like worms? Try them. Trust me—they're delicious!

You can even throw a party or wedding in our beautiful ballroom. Don't know how to dance? Don't lose your head over it. The only thing you should worry about is having fun.

So, are you ready to book a stay at the world's only hotel for monsters? What's that? You're not a monster?

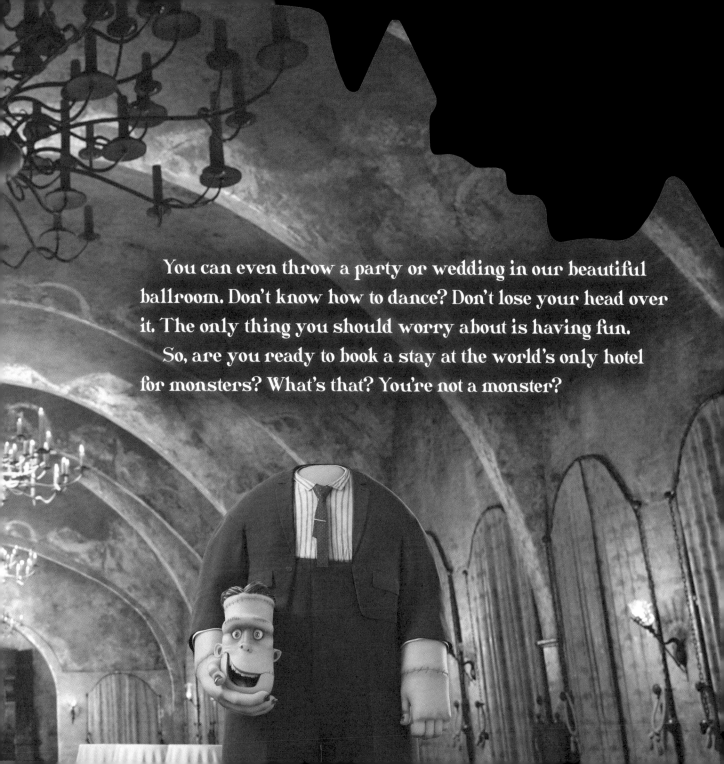

Silly me—I forgot to tell you the most important thing: Ever since Mavis fell in love with a human named Johnny, and they got married at this very hotel, and they had my grandson, Dennis, who is the light of my afterlife . . . the hotel is open to humans!

Enjoy your stay, and come again soon!

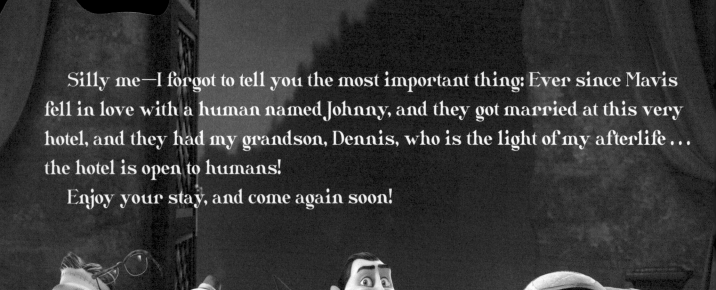